The Strange and Terrible Adventures of
POPOKI
THE HAWAIIAN CAT

Written by
Diana C. Gleasner

Illustrated by
Andrea Evans Winton

For POPOKI,
our beloved Hawaiian cat,
who has always had a mind of his own

© Copyright 1996
Second Printing 1997
PENINSULA PRESS
7994 Holly Court, Denver, NC 28037 U.S.A.

All Rights Reserved

Library of Congress Catalog Card Number: 96-92144

ISBN: 0-9651185-1-7

Printed in Hong Kong

Not so very long ago in a deep green valley on the island of Kauai lived a skinny kitten with a mind of his own.

"Scat!" The fisherman held the mahimahi away from the kitten.

The kitten kept his eyes on the fish. His ribs stuck out in furry bumps. He made a small, sad noise like a tiny baby's cry.

"Oh, Daddy," said Leilani. "He's starving. Poor thing." She tore off a piece of her peanut butter sandwich and held it out to the cat.

The kitten ate hungrily. He could not remember his last meal.

"Your Daddy hiked all the way into this valley to catch fish for our supper," Leilani's mother said. "He didn't catch it for a stray cat."

Leilani put her face against the cat's furry side. "He sounds like a motor," she said. "I can feel him purr."

When they left the valley, Popoki followed the scent of fresh mahimahi. Leilani's mother watched the kitten climb over huge rocks and scamper down a steep hill.

"He's full of spirit," she said. "A real Hawaiian Popoki."

"Popoki?" Leilani had never heard the word.

"It means cat," her mother explained. "They say a long time ago the missionaries used to call 'poor pussy, poor pussy.' When the Hawaiians tried to make those sounds, it came out 'Popoki'."

After that, Popoki lived in Leilani's garage in Hanalei Town.
Almost every day he caught a rat in the sugar cane field across
the road and proudly left it by the front door.

"Don't go into the field anymore," Leilani warned her cat one day. "It's almost ready for cutting. You might get hurt when they burn the cane."

Popoki had a mind of his own. He enjoyed rat hunting so
he went into the field anyway.

Popoki chased a mean and snarly rat through the cane. When he caught it, he tossed it around until he noticed tall yellow flames reaching toward the sky. Then he heard a roar like hundreds of cane-hauling trucks coming at him all at once. A great wall of fire flew up before him.

Popoki and the rat turned and ran the other way. They met another wall of flames. They were trapped! The rat did not stop. He ran right through the fire. Popoki followed. He could not see. He could not breathe. But he could run. Popoki had never run so fast. The ground was a blur. Flames were picking up speed. *The heat was terrible.*

He did not stop until he had crossed a stream. A large black cloud hung in the sky, but at last it was cool. His paws were very sore. He had never been so tired.

When he awoke, he spent a long time licking his singed fur and burned paws. The green cane field was gone. The rat was gone. Popoki was lost. He went back to sleep until hunger woke him up.

Popoki climbed steep cliffs, ran through fern jungles and thick groves of pandanus trees looking for something to eat. He did not know where he was, but he kept going.

The next day he came to a clearing that looked familiar.
Following a path that led down toward the ocean, he found
the valley that had been his first home.

Popoki drank from the clear cool stream. He even caught a small fish.

As the days went on, Popoki wondered about Leilani. He missed her.

Sometimes when his stomach was full, he would stop to admire towering waterfalls at the end of the valley or watch the rainbows come and go. The trouble was his stomach was almost never full.

One day while he was walking on the beach, he heard an awful noise, a siren so loud it hurt his ears. A boy threw down his fishing pole, grabbed Popoki and raced for a nearby hill. A man ran by them yelling, "Tsunami! Run for your life. A tidal wave is coming."

But Popoki had a mind of his own. He tried to wriggle
away but could not. So he scratched the boy on the arm.
The boy dropped Popoki and kept running.

The cat turned toward the ocean. All the water was backing away. Where the waves had always crashed onto the beach, fish flopped awkwardly on the wet sand. Something was very wrong.

Popoki knew he should run, but his stomach had a voice of its own and that voice said "Get those fish!"

Popoki was so busy trying to pick up a wiggly fish that he did not notice the ocean coming. A furious mountain of water picked him up. It tossed him about like a bit of fur in a crazy washing machine.

It carried him high up into the valley and threw him onto the top of a tall pandanus tree.

Bruised and confused, Popoki used every bit of his strength to hang on. All night the angry ocean surged into the valley.

All night he clung, wet and shivering, to the bouncy tree top.

In the morning he looked around. Some trees were gone.
They had been ripped right out of the ground by the waves.
Others, once tall and straight, leaned over and pointed
toward the ocean.

The beautiful green valley was ugly and brown, the color of mud.

After the night of the giant waves, there were not many fish in the stream. Popoki had to go far back into the valley for insects to keep him alive. When desperately hungry, he nibbled on soft pink guavas that lay rotting on the ground.

He slept in a cave, dreamed of mahimahi and whimpered
when he thought of Leilani.

   He decided to find her. After all, he was no longer a kitten.
He was a cat with a mind of his own, a mind that would listen
the next time he was warned about danger.

   A thin and scraggly Popoki limped through Hanalei Town on his way to Leilani's. When he finally found the house, he looked around. The cracked china bowl that had held his cat food was gone from the garage. The thick green cane field was bare and brown. No one was home. Exhausted from his journey, he dozed in the red ginger patch.

When Lielani came home from school, she found him.

   "Popoki! My poor pussy." Leilani scooped him up and
squeezed him so tightly he could hardly breathe. Then she took
the china bowl out of the cupboard and filled it with chunks of
fresh fish.

Popoki purred with pleasure. What could possibly be better than mahimahi for supper!